Lucy Goose Goes to Texas

Holly Bea
Illustrated by Joe Boddy

H J Kramer
Starseed Press
Tiburon, California

Art Director: Linda Kramer
Design and Production: Jan Phillips

Library of Congress Cataloging-in-Publication Data

Bea, Holly, 1956–
  Lucy Goose goes to Texas / by Holly Bea; illustrated by Joe Boddy. — 1st ed.
    p. cm.
  Summary: Lucy is a Canada goose who likes to do things by herself, but
when the time comes to migrate to Texas, she learns that there are good
reasons to work as a team. Includes information on the Canada goose.
  ISBN 1-932073-15-9 (hardcover : alk. paper)
 [1. Self-reliance—Fiction. 2. Individuality—Fiction. 3. Canada
goose—Fiction. 4. Geese—Fiction. 5. Stories in rhyme.] I. Boddy, Joe,
ill. II. Title.
PZ8.3.B3485Luc 2006
[E]--dc22

                              2005015138

H J Kramer
Starseed Press
P.O. Box 1082
Tiburon, California 94920

Printed in Singapore

10 9 8 7 6 5 4 3 2 1

For Michael Evan Weaver,
who is spreading his wings
— H.B.

For Erika and Jessika
— J.B.

This is Lucy. She lives in a shell.
It's smooth and it's white and she knows it so well.
It's cozy inside; she's toasty and warm.
Her needs are all met, and she's safe from all harm.

But something has happened — can you see a crack?
Her home has grown larger; there's no looking back.
She sees sunshine, a lake, and soft, fuzzy friends,
Three brothers, a sister, and a river that bends.

Her mother is gentle and shows them the way.
They learn how to waddle, to eat grass, and play.
They all listen closely and learn how to speak.
Lucy says, "Honk!" but it sounds more like "Peep."

Her mom says, "Don't worry! You'll grow big and loud.
You'll learn how to fly, and you'll make your mom proud.
Now it's time for Goose School; let's all jump in the river!
You've got work to do with your brothers and sister."

While all of the goslings would swim in a row,
That's not the direction that Lucy would go.
And when they would stretch their wings up toward the sky,
Lucy'd be watching a frog swimming by.

When the others went east, Lucy always went west.
She never seemed happy to stay with the rest.
Each day she would dream about learning to fly,
And what she would see of the world from the sky.

One day her mom called them down to the lake.
"It's time to discuss the big trip that we'll take.
When the weather gets cool and the leaves start to fall,
We'll head down to Texas and have us a ball!

"We go there each winter; it gets too cold here.
We'll leave before long, when the first frost appears.
We'll flap and we'll fly and we'll travel for days.
We'll all stick together 'cause that's the goose way.

"You'll see frost in the mornings and sunsets of red,
Snow-covered mountains and dry riverbeds.
There'll be bayous and orchards and aqua-blue streams;
It's the most beautiful country that you've ever seen.

"And when you reach Texas, why, you'll be surprised,
At tumbleweeds, cowboys, and wide-open skies.
Those Texans all love us when we come each year.
When we start to land, they'll give us a cheer!"

But Lucy had other ideas in her head.
"I'll fly alone, despite what Mom said.
I can't be the best if I fly in a pack.
I'm flying alone, and I'm not looking back."

While all the other geese worked hard together,
She kept to herself and liked it much better.
The others all said, "It's not easy alone,
When you're flying so long and so far from your home.

"Come fly in our V and we'll help you along."
But Lucy was sure that the others were wrong.
"I'm going to Texas! Just little ol' me!
And I'll get there first — just wait and you'll see!"

First thing in the morning, she started her flight.
"To Texas! To Texas!" she honked with delight.
Over meadows and valleys and rivers she flew,
Over houses and cities and traffic jams too.

She was alone, as she wanted to be,
But it wasn't much fun without company.
"If only my sister could see what I see;
If only my brothers could be here with me."

Then the wind started blowing; it was harder to fly.
Lucy got tired and wanted to cry.
"I'm cold and I'm hungry; I'm lonely and blue.
I'm all by myself. Oh, what will I do?
If only I'd listened and flown with the others . . .
I made a mistake; oh, I miss my mother."

She landed below, by an icy-cold river.
"Oh, what have I done?" she asked with a shiver.
"Maybe flying alone wasn't smart after all."
And from deep in the forest she heard a long howl.

"Oh no! What was that?" She was scared as could be.
"Now what's going to happen to little ol' me?"
She was frightened and cold and too tired to fly.
"I'll never reach Texas," she said with a sigh.

Then off in the distance she heard a small sound.
She looked high and low and then all around.
It sounded like honking — oh wait, could it be?
Look! There in the distance — could that be a V?

Yes, there were her friends! There was her mother!
They honked and they honked and came down with a flutter.
They said, "Come with us! Come fly in our V.
There's a reason we do it; come along and you'll see.

"We all get a lift when we fly in a V;
We don't get so tired; we fly easily.
It's all about teamwork; we all stick together,
So we get where we're going, no matter the weather.

"We honk at each other to say, 'You can do it!'
When we work as a team, we know we'll get through it.
So let's go to Texas where we all get to rest!
Let's all help each other to each be our best."

They flew in formation and honked all the way,
And they landed in Texas the very next day.
They saw wild armadillos and prairie dogs too,
Oil wells and longhorns and big skies of blue.

With her friends all around her, Lucy honked for attention.
"There's something important that I need to mention.
I learned a big lesson. It's all thanks to you.
I promise from now on I'll be tried and true.
I'm grateful I got to be part of the V.
I'm thankful you chose not to give up on me!"

The geese all honked loudly in wild celebration.
It was time to begin their big Texas vacation!
And the people all cheered as the geese settled in . . .
Lucy's winter adventure was about to begin!

Did You Know?

- Geese live near lakes, ponds, rivers, and grasslands.
- Geese like to eat grasses, corn, grains, and bugs.
- Once a male and female goose mate, they stay together for life.
- Female geese lay eggs in March or April, usually laying five to six white eggs.
- A baby goose is called a gosling.
- Goslings can swim as soon as they are born.
- Goslings learn to fly when they are nine to ten weeks old, after they grow their flight feathers.
- Geese migrate in the fall in search of food, which can become scarce during winter months in northern locations.
- Geese usually migrate to the same location each year.
- Geese fly in a V formation because it reduces the amount of wind resistance, making flying easier for each individual goose. As each bird flaps its wings, it creates uplift for the bird immediately following. The flock can increase its flying range by 71 percent by flying in a V formation.
- The goose at the head of the formation is called the lead goose. When the lead goose gets tired, he or she rotates to the back and another goose takes the lead position.
- When geese fly in a formation, they honk to encourage the lead goose.

Websites that provide additional information about Canada geese like Lucy:

- www.ducks.ca/naturenotes/cangoose.html
- www.kidzone.ws/animals/birds/canada-goose.htm
- www.gpnc.org/canada.htm